Anonymous

Transactions of the Nova Scotia Literary and Scientific Society

SALZWASSER
VERLAG

Anonymous

Transactions of the Nova Scotia Literary and Scientific Society

Reprint of the original, first published in 1859.

1st Edition 2022 | ISBN: 978-3-37513-394-8

Verlag (Publisher): Salzwasser Verlag GmbH, Zeilweg 44, 60439 Frankfurt, Deutschland
Vertretungsberechtigt (Authorized to represent): E. Roepke, Zeilweg 44, 60439 Frankfurt, Deutschland
Druck (Print): Books on Demand GmbH, In de Tarpen 42, 22848 Norderstedt, Deutschland

TRANSACTIONS

OF THE

NOVA-SCOTIA

LITERARY AND SCIENTIFIC SOCIETY,

JANUARY 4 TO DECEMBER 3, 1859.

HALIFAX, N. S.
PRINTED FOR THE SOCIETY, BY BOWES AND SONS.
1859.

CONTENTS.

OFFICE-BEARERS

OF THE

NOVA-SCOTIA LITERARY AND SCIENTIFIC SOCIETY,

FOR THE SESSION ENDING MAY, 1860.

Patron.

HIS EXCELLENCY THE RIGHT HON. THE EARL OF MULGRAVE,
LIEUT. GOVERNOR OF NOVA-SCOTIA, &c., &c.

President.

CHARLES COGSWELL, ESQ., M. D.

Vice-Presidents.

W. PRYOR, ESQ.   W. J. ALMON, ESQ., M. D.

Secretaries.

HUGO REID AND WM. GARVIE, ESQRS.

Treasurer.

S. L. SHANNON, ESQ., M. P. P.

Council.

T. B. AKINS, ESQ.	P. LYNCH, ESQ.
J. C. COGSWELL, ESQ.	A. MACKINLAY, ESQ.
W. A. HENRY, ESQ.	R. MORROW, ESQ.
P. C. HILL, ESQ.	H. PRYOR, ESQ., M. P. P.,
W. LAWSON, ESQ.	A. M. UNIACKE, ESQ.

INTRODUCTION.

FORMATION OF THE SOCIETY.

ON Tuesday, the 4th of January, 1859, a meeting, called by circular and notices in the newspapers, was held in No. 1 Dalhousie College, at 3 o'clock P. M., "to promote the formation of a Society, such as those established in other places, for the discussion of interesting and important questions in LITERATURE, SCIENCE, COMMERCE, and the ARTS."

On the motion of the Hon. STAYLEY BROWN, ANDREW MACKINLAY, Esq., President of the Mechanics' Institute, was called to the chair.

WM. GARVIE, Esq., was requested to act as Secretary to the meeting.

On the motion of HUGO REID, Esq., seconded by the Rev. Dr. CRAMP, it was

"*Resolved*, That a Society be established in this Province, to meet in Halifax, or at times in other places, for the reading and discussion of original communications on such subjects in LITERATURE, SCIENCE, POLITICAL ECONOMY, COMMERCE, STATISTICS, and THE ARTS, as may tend to draw forth talent and useful information; to encourage the study of the history, natural history, products and capabilities of the Province; to foster a spirit of enquiry and enterprise, and generally promote the advancement of science, learning, and the useful arts."

On the motion of ANDREW M. UNIACKE, Esq., seconded by Dr. COGSWELL, it was

"*Resolved*, That the gentlemen here present who enrol their names be members of the Society, and appoint the following gentlemen — with power to add to their number — to be a council or committee of management, to set the Society in action, frame regulations, and conduct the proceedings till December next, when they shall present a report to the first annual meeting of the members, at which the council for the ensuing year shall be chosen."

8

President.........	ANDREW MACKINLAY, Esq.
Vice-Presidents......	{ Rev. Dr. CRAMP, Principal of Acadia College. CHAS. COGSWELL, Esq., M. D.
Treasurer	S. L. SHANNON, Esq.
Secretaries.........	{ H. REID, Esq. W. GARVIE, Esq.

Council:

Hon. S. BROWN,
JAMES FORMAN, Esq.
J. C. COGSWELL, Esq.
W. A. HENRY, Esq.
Professor HENSLEY,
   King's College, Windsor.
P. C. HILL, Esq.
Professor HOW,
   King's College, Windsor.

Professor LYALL,
   St. John's College, Halifax.
PETER LYNCH, Esq.
JOHN NAYLOR, Esq.
D. McN. PARKER, Esq., M. D.
ALBERT PILSBURY, Esq.
WM. PRYOR, Esq.
Dr. ROBERTSON (Wilmot),
JAS. THOMSON, Esq.
ANDW. M. UNIACKE, Esq.

At the first meeting of Council, the following gentlemen were added to this list:—T. B. Akins, Esq., Dr. Gilpin, Lieut. Home, R. E., R. Miller, Esq., Lieut. Monro, R. A.

ORIGINAL MEMBERS.

At the meeting on the 4th of January, 1859, the following gentlemen enrolled their names as members of the Society :

Andrew Mackinlay,
C. Murdoch,
J. M. Cramp, D. D.,
J. C. Hume, M. D.,
H. Reid,
W. Garvie,
Andrew M. Uniacke,
F. G. D'Utassy,
Peter Lynch,
James Thomson,
G. Peple,

W. H. Tully,
S. Parker,
J. W. Johnston, jr.,
J. S. Thompson,
Hon. S. Brown,
Lieut. K. Munro, R. A.,
C. W. Dickson,
W. B. Smellie,
J. B. Campbell,
W. A. Henry.

OTHER MEMBERS.

The names of members subsequently added occur here in the order of their admission :—

S. L Shannon, M. P. P.
C. Cogswell, M. D.,
James Forman,
Rev. Prof. Lyall,
D. McN. Parker, M. D.,
J. Naylor,
A. Pilsbury, U. S. Consul.
W. Pryor,
P. C. Hill,
J. C. Cogswell,
T. B. Akins,
Lieut. Home, R. E.,
R. Miller,
Prof. Hensley, (Windsor),
Prof. H. How,   "
Rev. Dr. Robertson, (Wilmot),
B. Gilpin, M. D.,
Hon. John J. Marshall,
Hon. C. Tupper,
H. Pryor, M. P. P.,
W. Annand, M. P. P.,
A. K. Mackinlay,
W. S. Symonds,
W. Lawson,
Lieut. Duncan, R. A.,
R. Morrow,
C. W. H. Harris,
W. J. Almon, M. D.;
J. A. Graham,

E. A. Jones,
G. Buist,
W. Compton,
Rev. Dr. Forrester,
Hon. M. B. Almon,
H. Poole,
J. G. A. Creighton,
James Farquhar,
W. Murdoch,
W. H. Davis, M. D.,
J. N. Ritchie,
J. P. Lawson,
Hon. Judge Wilkins,
B. W. Hamilton,
J. H. Grigor,
F. Allison,
J. W. Nutting,
Rev. H. Bullock,
Rev. D. Honeyman,
C. P. Viale,
A. G. Archibald, M. P. P.,
R G. Haliburton,
E. G. Fuller,
James Woods,
H. Hartshorne,
His Lordship Hibbert Binney,
    Bishop of Nova Scotia.
F. Philpotts.

REGULATIONS.

NAME. The Society shall be called, THE NOVA SCOTIA LITERARY AND SCIENTIFIC SOCIETY.

OBJECTS. Its Objects shall be the study of the History, Natural History, and Resources of the Province, and generally the advancement of Science, Learning, and the Useful Arts.

MEMBERS. The Members shall be of three classes— ORDINARY, CORRESPONDING, and HONORARY.

Ordinary Members are admitted by the Council. They must be recommended by at least one member of the Society, and chosen by ballot at the meeting of Council following that at which they are proposed, by at least two-thirds of the members present.

The payments of Ordinary Members shall be Five Pounds on admission, constituting a Life Member; or One Pound on admission, to be reckoned for the current session, by gentlemen resident in Halifax; Ten Shillings by gentlemen in the country, and the same sums annually thereafter.

Gentlemen not residing in the Province may be elected *Corresponding Members*, and are to be admitted in the same manner as Ordinary Members, but are not called upon for any payment, so long as they reside beyond the bounds of the Province.

Gentlemen eminent for their literary or scientific attainments may be appointed *Honorary Members*; they shall be admitted in the same manner as Ordinary Members, except that they must be recommended in a written communication to the Secretaries, signed by at least five members of the Society. Honorary Members shall be exempted from all payments.

The business of the Society shall be conducted by the Council, who shall meet at such times as they think necessary, and shall have power to make Bye-laws, admit members, collect and disburse the funds, provide for the meetings of the Society, and generally do what is required to forward the objects of the Society.

An Annual Meeting of the members of the Society, to be called by circular and advertisement in two papers, will be held in the month of May.

At this Annual Meeting the Council shall present for approval a Report of the proceedings of the Society during the past session, any Bye-laws passed during the preceding year, and a financial report audited by two members of the Society, and any other business which they consider it necessary to refer to the members.

At this meeting office-bearers for the ensuing year shall be chosen by ballot.

The office-bearers shall be a President, two Vice-Presidents, a Treasurer, two Secretaries, and ten other Members of Council.

Their *term* of office shall expire at the Annual Meeting, but they may be re-elected.

On the requisition in writing, stating the object of the meeting, of five members, the President or Secretaries shall summon a Special Meeting of the Members of the Society, of which a week's notice shall be given (the business being specified in the circular) to consider and determine only upon the business mentioned in the requisition.

Members desiring to propose any alteration of the Regulations at the Annual Meeting, shall give intimation in writing to the Secretaries at least a fortnight before the meeting, that the members may have notice of the proposed alterations in the circular calling the meeting.

The Treasurer shall collect the payments due by the Ordinary Members, and present an Annual Report of the state of the funds, to be laid before a meeting of Council held previous to the Annual Meeting, and audited by members appointed at that meeting of Council. He shall make payments only on order by the Council, signed by the President or Vice-President, and the Secretaries.

The Secretaries shall summon, and take Minutes of the meetings of the Society and of the Council, and issue notices announcing the business at the meetings of the Society.

PAPERS READ DURING THE FIRST SESSION.

THE FOLLOWING PAPERS WERE READ BEFORE THE SOCIETY DURING ITS FIRST SESSION:—

Feby. 31, 1859.   1.—Opening Address of the PRESIDENT.

2.—On the kind of Education best suited for Nova Scotia.   By Dr. COGSWELL, Vice-President.

March 7.   Notes on the Preservation of Timber Buildings from Fire. By LIEUT. HOME, R. E.

March 21.   Decimal Currency.—By Hon. W. A. HENRY, M. P. P.

April 4.   The Fossiliferous Rocks of Arisaig, Sydney Co., N. S.— By Rev. D. HONEYMAN.

April 18.   Warming and Ventilation.—By W. S. SYMONDS, Esq.

May 2.   1.—A Communication from Prof. HOW, *King's College*, on certain new Minerals discovered by him, occurring in the Trap Formation, Bay of Fundy, N. S.

2.—The advantages of Local Museums in connection with Mineralogical Studies.—By H. POOLE, Esq.

ABSTRACT OF DR. COGSWELL'S PAPER.

Dr. Cogswell read a paper " *On the kind of Education best suited for Nova Scotia.*"

There had long been a depressed state of feeling prevailing in the Province with regard to its climate and resources, which the author attributed chiefly to the circumstance that the education of the people had not been of the best kind to make them acquainted with their own country, in consequence of which they had been governed by opinions emanating from the other side of the Atlantic, where the education was also defective as conveying but very slender information respecting the Colonies. In proof of this he referred to the school histories and geographies imported from England and commonly used in the Province, but treating so slightly of the Colonies that of late it was the practice to supply their deficiencies by special treatises; and yet these were the guides deemed sufficient in the mother country, so that there an individual might arrive at the highest honors of Oxford and Cambridge, without necessarily knowing anything of the various countries composing the empire, and which he might, in due course, aspire to rule over. In this Province our education had been framed on the English model, Windsor being our Oxford, where the leading and, till lately, the sole ambition, was to shine in the classics and mathematics. The author gave due credit to the eminent founders of Windsor College, a kind of institution necessary to qualify the few for the study of the learned professions; and he also thought it not desirable to interfere with the other denominational colleges, especially as each persuasion wished and was entitled to have a separate seminary to educate its own ministers. But for the mass of the people of a new country demanding practical minds and strong muscles to develop its capabilities, a system which tended to direct the thoughts exclusively into literary and abstract channels, was decidedly a mistake. There had been much discussion about the intention of the late Lord Dalhousie in founding the College called after his name, in which the Society were now assembled. His lordship's expressed wish was that it should be conducted " on the plan of the University of Edinburgh," which some interpreted in a theological sense, whereas proof existed that what he meant was to provide classes of practical instruction, open to all, without any religious test.

The author went into detail on the climate, soil, productions, and population of the Province. The climate, though a proverb in England of dreariness and inhospitality, by no means deserved its bad name, the thermometer being below zero only a few scattered days in winter, and never descending so low as even at Boston and New York—a fact lately brought into prominent notice by the telegraph. The soil in some of our Western Counties was superior, according to the best authority, to that of any State in the Union, not excepting the famous bottom land of Ohio. But the farmers were not taught to work systematically or to take sufficient pride in their occupation. The fisheries were the envy of foreigners, and yet, strange to say, the destitution of the " poor fishermen" of Nova Scotia was a standing topic at the great religious meetings in England, where there were actually several depôts for receiving "parcels of clothing for Newfoundland and Nova Scotia." These same fishermen were, physically, the pride of the Province, and were second to none in America for prowess at the oar. What they wanted was instruction to turn their efforts to the best account, and

habits of greater economy and foresight. The mineral resources were remarkably rich, especially in coal and iron.
For many years they were mostly in the hands of the Duke
of York's creditors, which perhaps would not have hap-
pened had our former leading men possessed the right kind
of knowledge to enable them to understand their value.
This monopoly was now, to a great extent, removed, and
a surprising spirit of enterprise was manifesting itself in
consequence. A chief cause of the bad repute of the Province was the selection of Halifax by Government for the site
of the capital, as, notwithstanding the noble harbour, the
ruggedness of the soil produced a bad impression on visitors.
The leading vessel of the fleet which brought Cornwallis and
his veterans to form the settlement was appropriately named
the *Sphinx*, for the Province had been a riddle to its people
and the world ever since. The natural capital, as shown by
the choice of Annapolis by the early settlers, was on the other
side of the Province. Fortunately, under the influence of
better opportunities for comparison, and an improved style of
education, more correct ideas were taking hold of the public
mind. Although the climate was unsurpassed for salubrity,
as shown especially by the Army medical returns, the training of the young had formerly seemed as if it were especially
contrived to ruin the health. The close, ill-ventilated school-
rooms, ill-provided with even decent accessories,—the absence
of play-grounds,—the long and monotonous hours of attend-
ance,—the scanty clothing of the children, especially those
of the weaker sex, partly with the false idea of making them
hardy, partly under the dictation of fashion, and the prefer-
ence given to luxurious over wholesome diet, were all repre-
hensible. These things were recently in process of reform
under the late and present able superintendents of education.
The leisure time of the young, once wasted in idleness and
dissipation, was now more generally employed in active

sports. At some of the schools the pupils were proficient in the military drill. Cricket was becoming universal. The Halifax Cricket Club, who enjoyed a rare privilege in having among their competitors the flower of the British youth belonging to the garrison and the ships-of-war on the station, had speedily shown themselves to be not unworthy of that distinction.

Nova Scotians used to charge themselves with being peculiarly wanting in enterprise. The Shubenacadie Canal was commonly quoted as an instance, but, in the author's opinion, it was rather an example of enterprise anticipating the demand for it. Its failure for a time had many remarkable parallels in the mother country. But look at the proofs of our commercial enterprise. In maritime pursuits Nova Scotia stood at the head of all the Colonies, and the Provincial tonnage far exceeded that of the whole Eastern Colonies put together. With the above material advantages, and others connected with their geographical position, and with a natural energy so evidently capable of doing these justice if rightly guided, Nova Scotians, instead of having reason to despond, had everything to cheer and encourage them. The author referred to the projected railroad to Canada and the Pacific, which would at once tend to enrich the Province by making it, like New York, a great thoroughfare to the West. The idea of this enterprise appeared to have originated with Nova-Scotians.

As a means of elevating the industrial pursuits and rendering them more attractive to young persons debating as to their choice of an occupation, the author spoke highly of an institution he had seen in England called a "Farmers' Club." Our farmers were separated from Halifax by a wide unproductive tract, and in coming to market felt themselves strangers in their own capital; but such an institution would tend to destroy the social barrier, and render agriculture a more honored and congenial pursuit. The primitive shed used for the sale of fish was unworthy of a prosperous city which prided itself on having the "finest fish market in the world." There should be a new building erected, and it might contain accommodation for an institution for the fishermen, corresponding to that proposed for the farmers. A school of practical instruction in mining operations,—and a board of examination to give certificates to masters of merchant vessels — were also recommended. By such means, superadded to the more sensible physical and moral training which was now in progress, the learned professions would cease to offer the only eligible openings to young men of wealth and social standing, and the great unimproved resources of the Province would put forward in an attractive light their just claims on the cultivated skill and energies of the population.

ABSTRACT OF A PAPER ON THE FOSSILIFEROUS ROCKS OF ARISAIG.

By REV. DAVID HONEYMAN.

THE Fossiliferous Rocks of Arisaig form a subject interesting in itself, interesting in its bearing on the Geology of Nova Scotia in particular, and on the science of Geology in general. They extend from Arisaig, which lies about fourteen miles south-west of Cape George, to Moydart, and are exposed on the shore from near Arisaig Pier to a little distance to the east of McAra's Brook, the extent of the exposure being nearly two miles, with a few interruptions.

This section is very interesting throughout, but the point of greatest interest is its western extremity, where the rocks in question meet with the carboniferous conglomerate, where they are only slightly metamorphic, and where the organisms which record the history and determine the relative age of this and similar rocks in the Province, are found in a remarkable state of preservation.

The metamorphosis of this section of rocks has resulted, probably, from the general volcanic action to which the metamorphic rocks of this period have been subjected, as well as from local and more recent volcanic action, of which there is here ample evidence.

These rocks are composed of layers of shale loose and more compact; this shale is generally argillaceous, and is often interstratified with limestone ; the shale is often fossiliferous. The limestone is rich in fossils, and appears chiefly to owe to these its existence.

The inhabitants of this petra present a somewhat motley appearance; their general aspect is unusual; their dresses are varied; one kind of stuff, the oxide of iron, has been used by nature in colouring their dresses, and yet they are attired in red, black, brown, grey and parti-color.

Although now inhabitants of the dry land, they were once tenants of the mighty deep, and may, therefore, be arranged as such — as Polyparia, Stellarida, Conchifera, Mollusca, Pisces.

We pass over the lowest class at present, and direct attention to the Stellarida — star-fishes.

Of these we have two very interesting representatives — a Uraster and a Crinoid. The Uraster is different from any of the five figured and described in Murchison's Siluria. The original cast was given to Dr. Dawson and a wax impression retained. It bears a striking resemblance to the common star-fish of our coasts, and doubtless the habits of the ancient corresponded with those of the modern.

To remains of the Crinoid star-fish a saintly origin has been ascribed, and to these the name St. Cuthbert's Beads has been given.

> " On a rock by Lindisfarm,
> St. Cuthbert sits and toils to frame
> The sea born beads that bear his name.
> Such tales had Whitby's fishers told,
> And said they might his shape behold,
> And hear his anvil sound —
> A deaden'd clang, a huge dim form,
> Seen but and heard when gathering storm
> And night were closing round."
> —MARMION.

At Arisaig, too, and upwards of 3,000 miles from Lindisfarm, St. Cuthbert's Beads are found in abundance, where the Saint's huge dim form is not seen, and where the deadened clang of his anvil is not heard. By the naturalist the reputed beads are regarded as the vertebræ of a Crinoid, or lily-like animal which lived attached to the rocks of the seas of the Transition and Carboniferous periods—an animal elaborate in its structure and wondrous in its beauty, and, as the sand on the sea-shore, innumerable. There are also abundance of Tentaculites, which are regarded as fingers of Crinoids. These star-fishes are, therefore, well represented in the number of their remains, although not in their variety.

The next class of organic remains to be examined is Conchifera—order, Monomyaria—family, Brachiopoda, (Lamarck.) This family is thus defined by Sowerby: "Bivalve adhering to marine bodies by a tendon passing through the shell, having no true ligament. What most distinguishes this family and renders it remarkable is the structure of the animal. It has two elongated, tendril-shaped arms. When the animal is in a state of repose these arms are coiled up spirally and enclosed in the shell, but when required for use, are unfolded and extended."

Belonging to this family we have at Arisaig—Atrypa, Producta, Terabratula, Spirifera. Of these the most characteristic are Atrypa affinis, Producta depressa, and Spirifer elevatus. Of Orthidiform Conchifers there is great abundance; moderns of this character are generally brought from depths of from sixty to ninety fathoms. According to the testimony of these rocks the Brachiopod Conchifers were the most numerous of the testaceous inhabitants of the seas in which they were formed.

The next class to which attention is directed is Mollusca univalve—order, Trachelipoda (Lam.) Of these we present Euomphalus, Turbo Williamsi, (?) Holopella obsoleta, H. cancellata, H. gregaria. The Spiral univalves are here comparatively few in number and small in size.

The next univalve to which we would refer is named Bellerophon, after the heaven-aspiring and ill-fated rider of the

2

winged Pegasus. This fossil has been referred by Lamarck to the order Monothalamous Cephalopoda, of which there exists one genus — Argonauta. Murchison refers it to the order Heteropoda. The modern Heteropod, is a floater swimming in a reversed position, the fin-like foot being uppermost, and the shell depending; they are limited to warm latitudes. One species of the genus Carinaria, the modern genus of this order of Molluscs, inhabits the Mediterranean, and occasionally appears on particular coasts in large numbers, whilst others are peculiar to the tropics, where most of the allied genera also exist. Of the Bellerophon there are six species in the Arisaig rocks; we have been able to determine four of these — B. Murchisoni, B. expansus, B. trilobatus, B. carinatus.

The last order of Mollusc univalve to which we direct attention is the Polythalamous cephalopoda, (Lam.) The name has been given on account of the many chambers of which the shell or float of this order of univalve is composed, and because they have their feet or locomotive organs arranged round the head.

This is to be regarded as the highest order of Molluscs on account of the complexity of their organization and the nearness of its approach to that of the vertebrated animals. In the general form of their bodies many members of this class bear a strong resemblance to fish. They have eyes and organs of hearing like the higher classes of animals; their feet are also to be considered as arms, for they are prehensile as well as locomotive ; these feet or arms are from eight to ten in number, and in some cephalopods they are said to number nearly 100. They are covered with suckers like the leathern ones of the urchin, by which they can take a firm hold of any thing to which they may be applied in walking or in hunting ; their mouth is situated in the centre of this locomotive or prehensile apparatus, and consists of a pair of horny mandibles resembling the bill of a parrot, which is provided with a large fleshy tongue, rough with thorny prickles. Prof. R. Jones thus eloquently describes the action of a cephalopod: "Let the Poulpe touch its prey, it is enough; once a few of these tenacious suckers get firm hold, the swiftness of the fish is unavailing, as it is soon trammelled on all sides by the firmly holding tentacula, and dragged to the mouth of its destroyer. The shell 6f the lobster and crab is a vain protection, for the hard and crooked beak of the cephalopod easily breaks to pieces the frail armor."

The shell of the Polythalamous Cephalopod has also a siphuncle or tube opening through its chambers and connecting them together; this siphuncle is sometimes shelly, as in the float of the Spirula Peronii, of which we have several specimens, or membraneous, as in the Nautilus Pompilius. By this wonderful contrivance the cephalopod of this order is enabled to walk about at the bottom of the sea, and to raise and sink itself with ease and comfort. In some cases the shell serves for a dwelling and float, as with the Nautilus; sometimes it is partly internal, or contained in the body of the animal, e. g. in the Spirula Peronii; and again it is sometimes internal, e. g. in the cuttle-fish, and hence it is vulgarly called the cuttle-fish bone.

We only refer in the present paper to one variety of a fossil of this order, found in the Arisaig rocks, reserving others more interesting, for a future communication. The specimens in question are Orthocerata. Were a nautilus shell uncoiled and straightened, an Orthoceras would be produced, with a somewhat too commodious upper chamber. The plainest appears to be the Orthoceras laterale. We have not been fortunate enough to meet with a gigantic specimen of this cephalopod, such as that met with at Closeburn, near Edinburgh, which is said to be as thick as a man's leg; but we have met with specimens of various dimensions, some of them tolerably large, with about thirty chambers. Many of them appear to be perfect, but in no circumstance is the upper chamber such as could have accommodated the ancient proprietor, so that they must either have only partially accommodated their possessors, or have been partially internal, like the float of the spirula.

The Orthocerata occur until the formation of the carboniferous or mountain limestone.

They were thus early called into being by the *fiat* of their Creator; they then occupied a prominent place in the testacea of the ocean, and early and entirely disappeared.

We are therefore to consider these and their congeners as analogues of existing cephalopods, and to regard their general offices as the same; to regard them as enemies of the finny tribes, for there is evidence that such existed, even then; as the enemy of the crustacea, which we shall yet have occasion to show did then abound; as the destroyer of the Brachiopod and Trachelipod; and, in the absence of Carnivorous Trachelipods, they appear to have been more numerous than they otherwise would have been, or than the cephalopods are in the present day, being the principal ministers of Providence destined to regulate the numbers of the testaceous population of those ancient seas. Wherever the crustacea especially abound, these cephalopods present themselves; sometimes we find their remains in closest juxtaposition, suggesting the beautiful stanza:

> " There servants, masters, small and great,
>   Partake the same repose,
>   And there in peace the ashes mix
>   Of those who once were foes."

The last class of organic remains to which attention is directed, is Crustacea. Of this class of creatures the lobster and crab are familiar examples. The Oniscus or "Slater,"

as we were wont to call it in Scotland, more strikingly repre-
sents the form of the Arisaig Crustacea, with the exception of
the Beyrichia, which is a bivalve Crustacean; these are
abundant.

The other crustacea which resemble considerably the Slater,
are Trilobites — so called from the three-fold division of their
dorsal crust. This division is in general obvious — sometimes
obscure. Almost every schoolboy has seen the figure of the
Trilobite Calymene Blumenbachii, known also as the Dudley
Trilobite, or he may see it by referring to Geology in Chambers' Introduction to the Sciences. This trilobite is very
common in the Arisaig rocks; of this we have found heads
and tails varying from two lines to one and a-half inches.
Entire trilobites of this and every kind are here very rare
indeed. We have, after a five years' search, met with only
one whole specimen, and our consequent joy on its discovery
was not less than that of Archimedes, on the occasion of his
well-known exclamation, " Eureka, eureka !" The pupils of
the eyes of this trilobite have not, in any case, been preserved.
This is a fossil of the Wenlock limestone and upper Ludlow
rock.

The trilobite Homalonotus presents two varieties, the tail
of the one having a long peak, the tail of the other being
without it. We have two specimens of tails of the one, and
about seventy tails of the other; some of these are of considerable size, and there are also heads corresponding, and
abdominal fragments; the eyes have shared the same fate as
those of the Dudley Trilobite. The discovery of the Homalonotus in so great a number, appears to solve an important
problem of Nova Scotia Geology.

Lyell says, in his Elementary Geology, (Ed. 4th, p. 354):
" The Homalonotus delphino-cephalus is common to this
division (lower Ludlow shale) and to the Wenlock limestone.
This crustacean belongs to a group of trilobites which has been

met with in the Silurian rocks only, and in which the tripartite character of the dorsal crust is almost lost."

We have next a trilobite which is probably a variety of the Asaphus. Of this we have also heads and tails in abundance. Some of the heads are well preserved so as to reveal the eyes, which have been characterized as "among the most' wonderful of the revelations of Geology." These eyes are composed of facets like the eyes of the house and dragon fly, and are placed in such a manner as, though fixed, to survey the circle of surrounding objects. Fossil anatomists have affirmed that there are 400 of such facets in a single eye of the Asaphus; we have not been able, in almost perfect specimens, to reckon more than 120, but even this is a respectable number. We quote the admirable observations of Buckland on this subject: " Besides the above analogies there remains a still more important point of resemblance in the structure of their eyes. This point deserves peculiar consideration, as it affords the most ancient and almost the only example in the fossil world of the preservation of parts so delicate as the visual organs of animals that ceased to live many *thousands*, and perhaps, *millions* of years ago. We regard these eyes with feelings of no ordinary kind when we recollect that we have before us the identical instruments of vision through which the light of heaven was admitted to the sensorium of some of the first created inhabitants of our planet.

" With respect to the waters wherein the trilobites maintained their existence throughout the entire period of the Transition formation, we conclude that they could not have been that imaginary, turbid, and compound chaotic fluid from the precipitates of which some Geologists have supposed the materials of the surface of the earth to be derived, because the structure of the eyes of these animals is such that any kind of fluid in which they could have been efficient at the bottom must have been pure and transparent enough to allow the passage of light to organs of vision the nature of which is so fully disclosed by the state of perfection in which they are preserved.

" With regard to the atmosphere, also, we infer that, had it differed materially from its actual condition, it might have so far affected the rays of light that a corresponding difference from the eyes of existing crustaceans would have been found in the organs on which the impressions of ·such rays were then received. Regarding light itself, also, we learn from the resemblance of these most ancient organizations to existing eyes, that the mutual relations of light to the eye and of the eye to light, were the same at the time when crustaceans endowed with the faculty of vision were first placed at the bottom of the primeval seas, as at this moment. Thus we find among the earliest organic remains an optical instrument of most curious construction, adapted to produce vision of a peculiar kind, in the then existing representatives of one great class of the articulated division of the animal kingdom. We do not find this instrument passing onwards, as it were, through a series of experimental changes from more simple into more complex forms ; it was created, at the very first, in the fullness of perfect adaptation to the uses and condition of the class of creatures to which this kind of eye has ever been and is still appropriate."

There have also been found a very few remains of fish near two or three Orthocerata.

We therefore draw the following inferences :

1.—Prof. E. Forbes, in accordance with his theory, would have regarded the Arisaig rocks as of deep-sea origin. (Vide Lyell's El. Geol., 4th Ed., p. 360.)

2.—The climate of this region at the time of the deposition of these rocks, was equivalent to a tropical climate.

3.—The prevalence of the Calymene Blumenbachii and Homalonotus and the general resemblance of the fossils to those of the upper Ludlow rock, show that these rocks are of upper Silurian age, or of the second era of organic existence.

Our imagination takes its flight;—in ages long gone we exist;—in old ocean's still abyss, at a depth of seventy fathoms, we take our stand. We survey below, above, and around us; there is life, activity and beauty. The Star-fish is bestirring itself; he expands his rays; he protrudes his feet; he advances and climbs in search of his testaceous food. The Crinoid, whose name is legion, of varied size and beauty, with foot firmly attached to the rock, exercises its numerous joints and plies its busy fingers in search of food, or in conveying the tiny morsel to its proper receptacle. The Conchifers innumerable—Atrypa, Producta, Terebratula, Spirifera, employ the instruments furnished by a kind Providence for their support and enjoyment. The Mollusc tribe are all engaged in their proper spheres. The Petillæ or Limpets adhere to the rocks for protection or comfort, or move on with sluggish pace, in search of provision. The Trochidæ advance with their attached habitations in search of vegetable food, or at the approach of an enemy withdraw into their convenient dwellings and shut the aperculum, or door, behind them. The numerous Crustacea—Beyrichia, Asaphus, the marvellous eyed Calymene or Homalonotus—in swarms rest themselves, paddle about, cautiously approach a defunct Orthoceras, or feast upon its carcase. Bellerophonta on all sides pervade the briny deep. Orthoceras and his congeners with elevated float, walk about and devour Gasteropods, Trachelipods and Conchifers, or dash among the Crustacea, spreading consternation around, or fasten upon and entrammel the light and swift fish—the shell of the testacea, the coat of mail of the trilobite, and the spine of the fish, forming a vain protection. In conclusion, we see generation after generation becoming extinct—entombed in the clay of the ocean's bed—this bed, by mechanical and chemical agencies converted into successive layers of rock—shoals of conchifers and their contemporaries, by means of their houses, forming interstratified limestone. We see nature, by chemical constituents of these rocks, oftentimes embalming their entombed inhabitants as no Egyptian physician could embalm; not to present, after a few thousand years, a dry and withered mummy, but, after years whose numbers we cannot imagine, to present them almost, if not altogether, as lovely as when they were at first entombed. Finally, we see this era of organic existence come to an end. Vulcan stirs his central fires—the rocks are melted, the earth is convulsed; the rocks are rent, and from far below the ocean's bed they are raised to threaten the sky. The Himmalayas, the Andes, the Alleghanies, the Cobequid, &c., come into being; the entombed inhabitants of the ocean are elevated above its level to heights oftentimes inaccessible; their tombs are made to adorn the earth, and with other rocks to declare the might and majesty of their Maker, and minister to the necessities and wants of him who is made in the image of the Invisible; their organisms are made to show forth the glory of GOD, and to minister to man's instruction.

DESCRIPTION AND ANALYSIS OF THREE NEW MINERALS, ASSOCIATES IN THE .TRAP OF THE BAY OF FUNDY.

By Prof. Henry How,

OF KING'S COLLEGE, WINDSOR, NOVA-SCOTIA.

The minerals of which I propose giving an account in the present paper, were found in June, 1858, by Dr. Webster of Kentville, N. S., and myself, in the trap rock of the Bay of Fundy, on the shore of Annapolis County, N. S., a couple of miles or so east of a headland called Black Rock, which is well-known to the navigators of the Bay from being of considerable height and jutting some distance into the water.

On this occasion in our search for specimens we landed about a mile east from Black Rock and walked eastwards; which circumstance I mention because it afforded us an opportunity of observing the nature of the rock under which we travelled. As is well-known to those who have visited these shores, the Bay of Fundy presents on the Nova Scotian side three varieties of trap, viz., the tufaceous, the vesicular amygdaloidal, and the more compact crystalline rock. The cliffs under which we passed for some distance had the last-named character, being dark blue-black in colour, as indicated in the name Black Rock, frequently perpendicular, and showing little evidence of recent action of water and frost, from the absence of any fragments but such as were small, worn smooth, and rounded by long attrition on the beach. I do not remember having observed any columnar structure. We experienced the known barrenness of this kind of rock in specimens, having obtained comparatively few in a toilsome journey; the specimens were principally apophyllite and lammonite; among those we found, however, were the subjects of this communication.

These minerals composed the mass of a solid, uniform nodule about half the size of a fist, partly imbedded in the crystalline trap adverted to above. The nodule was covered over the greatest part of its surface with a dark, green coating, spangled with crystals, apparently of chlorite; the portion free from this coating showed irregularly hemispherical protuberances of a yellowish colour and stellated appearance. The nodule yielded with difficulty to the hammer, and when broken presented a curious internal structure.

Immediately below the thin, green coating was observed a narrow band of yellowish-white mineral resembling wax, isolated patches of which, few in number, occurred a little removed from the rind, among spherical concretions having a most distinct stellated appearance, and, in portions, a highly pearly lustre, while the centre was principally made up of a bluish-white, opaque-looking mineral in rounded spots. The components of the nodule were so closely packed that only one very small cavity was observed, the margins of which had a radiated structure.

The only difficulty experienced in determining the nature of this mass was in the separation of its constituents, which, from their very intimate association, proved an extremely tedious process; while, from their containing the same elements in different proportions, great care was requisite to ensure trustworthy results on analysis.

Cyanolite, the mineral mentioned as most abundant in the centre of the nodule, was found to present no crystalline structure. Its hardness $=4.5$, very coherent in the mass, rather brittle than tough in small pieces; S. G. $=2.495$ in coarse fragments, fracture flat, conchoidal, even; streak, white; lustre, dull; colour, bluish-gray; subtranslucent in very thin pieces, translucent on the edges, powder transparent under the microscope. A fragment not altered in strong nitric acid; in powder did not gelatinize before or after ignition, but afforded slimy silica; in matrass became white, giving off water; before the blow-pipe in platinum forceps, the edges only of thin splinters were rounded in a good heat, with borax and with soda gave transparent beads, with salt of phosphorus, a translucent glass.

The results of the following analyses were obtained by first igniting the powdered mineral for water, and then treating the residue with strong H Cl, digesting and evaporating to dryness. The resulting silica, after being dried and weighed, was fused with carbonate of soda, the fused mass being decomposed by H Cl in the regular way, was found to yield very nearly the amount (under 0.8 per cent. less) of silica first obtained; the second weight was taken as the correct estimate, and the small quantities of alumina and lime now set free were determined and added to those from the first acid'fluid. This method, though rather tedious, served to economize a material not readily obtained in a state fit for analysis — one quantity furnishing a knowledge of all the constituents.

The results afforded by the *airdry* mineral, were:

	I.		OXYGEN.	RATIO.
Lime,	17·52	=	5·00	1
Alumina,	0·84		0·39	
Magnesia,	trace			
Potass,	0 53		0·09	
Silica,	74·15	=	39·28	7·85
Water,	7·39	=	6·56	1·31
	100.43			

A second experiment upon what I consider to be this

mineral less perfectly freed from that which will be next described, afforded :

II.

Lime, ...	18·19
Alumina, ...	1·24
Magnesia, ...	trace
Potass, ...	0·61
Silica, ...	72·52
Water, ...	6·91
	99·47

which numbers agree sufficiently well with the first, under the circumstances, to show definite composition, the formula expressive of which, however, I deduce from the first analysis. The alumina* and potass are evidently not essential constituents, and probably replace a portion of the lime ; the ratio of oxygen in the lime, silica, and water, as found, is 1 : 7·85 :,1·31 ; taking this as 4 : 31·40 : 5·2. I propose as the formula of Cyanolite :

$$4 \, CaO, \ 10 \, SiO_3 + 5 \, HO,$$

which requires the per centages :

$$4 \, CaO \ = \ 112 — 18·36$$
$$10 \, SiO_3 \ = \ 453 — 74·26$$
$$5 \, HO \ = \ 45 — 7·37$$
$$610 \quad 100·00$$

according satisfactorily with the result of experiment.

It is, perhaps, worth observation that, if the water be taken as basis, the ratio of oxygen in all the bases is to that of silica as 1 : 3·2, approximating to that in the anhydrous silicate of lime, Edelforsite, $CaO \, SiO_3$, in which it is 1 : 3.

I have named the mineral Cyanolite, in allusion to the blue tint which distinguishes it from its associates.

* Dana 4th Ed. I. p. 208.

Centrullassite. The association of this mineral with the preceding is very intimate. As already mentioned, Cyanolite was found most abundantly in the centre of the mass, in patches of a rounded outline, between which sometimes a transparent, sometimes an opaque white, substance was seen, the latter being, as afterwards shown, a condition of the former, both presenting a stellated appearance; towards the exterior of the nodule this character was very decided, so much so that I at first considered the mineral to be gurolite, which it resembles in some other points and approaches in composition.

Centrallasite lies next the rind mentioned before and to be fully described presently, and when free from it, shows elevations of a somewhat semi-globular external form, radiated on the surface; when broken, these are found to possess a lamellar structure, and to consist of plates diverging from a centre, forming truly spherical concretions; the surfaces of these plates have a highly pearly lustre, but the mineral passes into an opaque, white condition, by a change which appears to commence uniformly at the centre, or to proceed from point of contact with cyanolite; this state is seen in fractures of the interior of the nodule, and will be shown presently not to arise from efflorescence. The name chosen for the mineral is in allusion to this character. Centrallasite is white, sometimes yellowish, translucent, perfectly transparent in thin plates, which are easily obtained and readily broken across. It is rather brittle under the pestle, not difficult to powder; lustre resinous, highly pearly on cleavage planes; hardness $= 3.5$; S. G. $= 2.45\ 2.46$. In matrass yields water, becoming opaque and silvery white; does not exfoliate. Alone before the blow-pipe, fuses readily with continued spirting to an opaque, glassy bead; with soda, dissolves in considerable quantity to a transparent glass; with borax, affords a transparent bead; with phosphorus salt, dissolves slowly and entirely to a clear bead; a piece in strong nitric acid splits into translucent laminæ; in powder, readily acted upon by H Cl without gelatinizing; after ignition, affords flocculent silica on long digestion with the same acid.

Analysis afforded the following results. In No. 1 separate quantities were taken for water and for the other constituents; in No. 2 the mode described with reference to Cyanolite was adopted, and was found to render the amount of silica obtained by digestion of the ignited mineral by 1·5 per cent.; the last portions of water were not easily expelled; experiment was made on *airdry* material, viz., immediately after its being powdered.

	I.	II.	Mean.		Oxygen.	Ratio.
Lime, . . .	27·86	27·97	27·91	=	7·97	1
Alumina, . .	1·00	1·28	1·14	=	0·53	
Magnesia, . .	0·20	0·13	0·16			
Potass, . .	undet.	0·59	0·59	=	0·10	
Silica, . . .	59·05	58·67	58·86	=	31·18	3·91
Water, . .	11·40	11·43	11·41	=	10·14	1·27
	99·51	100·07	100·07			

I quote separately the results of another analysis, in which the portion of mineral ignited for water was employed for the determination of the other constituents, and the silica not subsequently fused with carbonate of soda; the numbers obtained were:

Lime, ...	27·09
Alumina, ...	0·40
Silica, ...	61·10
Water, ...	11·03
	99·62

which are of value, as showing that the amount of water is constant, and assuming the same quantity of silica, etc., to be rendered insoluble, that the other constituents have the relations observed in the preceding analyses, upon the results of which alone I base my conclusions regarding the formula. The Oxygen ratio of Ca O, Si O3, II O—evidently the essential components—is shown to be, 1 : 3·91 : 1·27 ; taking this as 4 : 15·64 : 5·08, I deduce, as the formula of Centrallasite :

$$4 \ CaO, \ 5 \ Si O_3, \ + \ 5 \ HO,$$

the percentages corresponding to which are :

$$
\begin{aligned}
4 \ CaO \ &= 112 \ &&-29\text{·}20 \\
5 \ Si O_3 \ &= 226\text{·}5 &&-59\text{·}06 \\
5 \ HO \ &= 45 \ &&-11\text{·}74 \\
\hline
&\ 383\text{·}5 &&100\text{·}00
\end{aligned}
$$

and with these the experimental numbers agree very well, upon the view that a small proportion of lime is replaced by the alumina, magnesia, and potass.

The formulas adopted for these two minerals exhibit a very simple relation existing between them, thus :

Cyanolite $= 4 \ CaO, \ 10 \ Si O_3 + 5 \ HO.$
Centrallassite $= 4 \ SiO, \ \ \ 5 \ Si O_3 + 5 \ HO.$

They differ by five equivalents of silica.

If, however, a part of the water in the analyses of the latter mineral be taken as a basis, a correspondence may be traced between it and Okenite ; thus the formula being written : Centrallassite $= (4 \ CaO, \ 3\frac{1}{2} \ HO,) \ 5 \ Si O_3 + 1\frac{1}{2}$ aq. $= 4$ CaO, $5 \ Si O_3 + 5 \ II O$—may be compared with that of Okenite, so written as to bring out the angcloid oxygen ratio* between bases and silica of 1 : 2, thus,

Okenite $= 3 \ (CaO, \ HO,) \ 4 \ Si O_3 + 3$ aq. $= 3 \ CaO,$ $4 \ Si O_3 + 6 \ HO.$

---

* Dana's Min., 4th Ed., pp. 301, 306, and Sixth Supplement to same in Silliman, Nov., 1558, p. 363.

In both we have the ratio of oxygen in bases and silica as
1 : 2; and further, while the chemical composition of centrallassite is nearer that of okenite than of gurolite, its mineralogical characters resemble those of the latter* closely in some
respects, and the lime and silica in its formula are those of
both these two together.

Okenite = 3 CaO, 4 Si O₃ + 6 H O ⎫ Centrallassite = 4 Ca O
Gurolite = CaO, Si O₃ + 1½ H O ⎭   5 Si O₃ + 5 H O.

The opaque condition of the mineral just described does not
depend on loss of water. As already mentioned, the concretions of pearly plates are sometimes observed to be chalk-
white towards the centre, and even in freshly exposed surfaces
of the interior of the nodule, spherical masses were seen, without lustre, chalk-white, and in which a radiated structure was
sometimes, but not invariably, quite obvious; on igniting a
selection of such fragments as appeared most characteristic,
the percentages of water in two cases were found to be

I.   II.
Water, = 12·29   12·25,

and the silica in the ignited residue of I. was found, by simple
action of H Cl, to amount to 61·11 per cent., or the same
quantity as obtained from the transparent mineral (analysis
III. ante.) under similar circumstances; these numbers satisfy
me as to the identity of the mineral. The amount of water
now exhibited is conclusive evidence that efflorescence had
not occurred, and although the slight excess over the previous
percentages may suggest the idea that hydration was in progress, it is difficult to imagine such a process taking place in
the interior of the nodule, where the opaque condition
appeared most perfectly developed, a situation in which the
only obvious means of such change lies in the transference of
water from cyanolite. In speaking of *change* occurring, I

---

assume that the transparent lamellar form is the more perfect condition of the mineral, and though it is possible that the opaque may also have been an original form of deposition, I am disposed to look upon the latter as really resulting from the former, possibly in consequence of some molecular action.

I must add that on one occasion a fracture of the nodule brought to view two very small tufts of divergent silky, transparent needles, which, when examined under the microscope, appeared to be sided prisms, and which had the blow-pipe characters of the pearly laminae; whence I conclude that the needles consist of centrallassite.

Cerinite. The narrow band already adverted to as enveloping the two preceding minerals was about an eighth of an inch in thickness, and portions having the same characters were observed in rounded concretions between masses of the centrallassite, (which was invariably next the band,) and in these a concentric structure in layers was seen. The mineral is opaque or subtranslucent in very thin fragments; it is amorphous, its powder exhibiting under the microscope a mass of transparent grains without crystalline form; its lustre subresinous, looking very like wax; white or yellowish white; hardness = 3·5; readily fusible without intumescence before the blow-pipe.

In the portion selected for the first of the following analyses, a few very minute red spots were visible, and it was scarcely possible to obtain the mineral *absolutely* free from its associates. The first analysis having shown that the mineral, after ignition, was very imperfectly attacked by HCl, and that fusion with carbonate of soda was necessary for its decomposition, this method was at once resorted to in the second case. The results afforded by the mineral, without artificial desiccation, were :

	I.	II.	Mean.	Oxygen.	Ratio
Lime, . . .	9·49	10·15	9·82 =	2·80	} 1
Magnesia, .	1·83	1·91	1·87 =	0·76	
Potass, . .	0·37*	undet	0·37		
Alumina, .	12·21	13·11	12·65 =	5·90	} 1·75
Peroxide of Iron,	1·01*	1·27	1·14 =	0·34	
Silica, . .	58·13	57·02	57·57 =	30·50	8·56
Water, . .	15·96	15·42	15·69 =	13·94	3·91
	99·00	98·88	99·21		

The loss in the analysis probably proceeds from alkalies not determined, and the ratio between KO, $K_2 O_3$, $Si O_3$ and HO, as exhibited, may be taken as $1 : 2 : 9 : 4$, which we have in the formula :

$$3 \, Ca O \, Si O_3, \, 2 \, (Al_2 O_3, \, 3 \, Si O_3) + 12 \, HO,$$

the percentage of which :

3 CaO,	.	.	.	84·00—11·96
2 Al₂ O₃,	.	.	.	102·52—14·60
9 Si O₃,	.	.	.	407·70—58·06
12 HO,	.	.	.	108·00—15·38
				702·22 100·00

correspond very well with the experimental numbers so far as $Si O_3$ and HO are concerned, and are tolerably close to the aggregate amounts of isomorphous constituents respectively.

No mineral of the same character and composition having been described, and taking the association into consideration, I look upon this as a new mineral combination, and have named it Cerinite, in allusion to its wax-like appearance. An examination of the formula assigned to the mineral shows it to contain the elements of Edelforsite with those of two equivalents of Stilbite.

---

* As dissolved by H Cl.

Edelforsite = $CaO\ SiO_3$.

$$\underline{2\ \text{Stilbite} = 2\ (CaO\ SiO_3 + Al_2O_3\ 3\ SiO_3 + 6\ HO.)}$$

Cerinite = $3\ CaO\ SiO_3 + 2\ (Al_2O_3\ 3\ SiO_3) + 12\ HO.$

The group of minerals now described appears to have been the result of deposition in this order; the cerinite being laid as a lining to the cavity of the trap rock, the centrallassite began to be formed, and then the aluminous material was virtually exhausted in the small patches of cerinite interspersed among the accruing deposit, while the centrallassite and cyanolite appear to have been formed in alternating actions.

As respects chemical composition, the two latter minerals are interesting additions to the known hydrated silicates of lime, of which two only have been hitherto described, viz., Okenite and Gurolite, and whether they are truly regarded as permanent species or not, they have a claim to our attention as ascertained products of the chemistry of inorganic nature; and this is, to my mind, true of all results of chemical investigation into natural operations, whether they prove, on complete study, to refer to intermediate or to final stages of chemical action—as, in the first case, contributing to our knowledge of the course of changes, and in the latter exhibiting their perfection.

The relations of the minerals now spoken of are shown by reducing their formulas to the same standard of comparison, which may be done by taking the same number of equivalents of lime, the base, in each case, in this manner:

Gurolite, $2\ (CaO\ SiO_3) + HO$, taken twice $= 4\ CaO,\ SiO_3 + 6\ HO.$
Okenite, $3\ CaO, 4\ SiO_3 + 6\ HO + \frac{1}{3}$ its formula $= 4\ CaO, 5\frac{1}{3}\ SiO_3 + 8\ HO.$
Centrallassite, ... $= 4\ CaO,\ 5\ SiO_3 + 5\ HO.$
Cyanolite. .... $= 4\ CaO, 10\ SiO_3 + 5\ HO.$

From which view it is obvious that both the latter have more silica in their composition than the other described hydrated silicates of lime ; and if we glance at the formulas of the two anhydrous silicates of lime,

$$\text{Wollastonite} = 3 \text{ Ca O, 2 Si O}_3,$$
$$\text{Edelforsite} = \text{Ca O Si O}_3,$$

we see that Cyanolite is by far the most highly silicated combination of lime yet met with. This new relation, of so decided a character, between lime and silica, familiar to us as partial components of mineral substances in various approximative proportions, appears to me to render Cyanolite especially interesting to mineralogists.

ABSTRACT OF MR. POOLE'S PAPER.

MR. HENRY POOLE read a paper on the Advantages to be derived from the Establishment of Museums for the Collection of Specimens in Practical Geology, and suggested that there should be one in every Court House throughout the Province, showing the mineralogical and geological specimens to be found in each County, and that there should be a central museum in Halifax, where duplicates from all the County museums might be grouped according to their geological positions.

He considered the present time favourable for bringing the subject under public notice, as the minerals of Nova Scotia had lately been thrown open to public enterprise; and also as a new Court House was being built, it would afford an opportunity for the appropriation of one of the rooms in the Province Building, and if his scheme were carried out he believed it would be the most attractive place in Halifax for visitors, and especially strangers, to resort to.

A small Provincial grant would cover all the expenses, and then it might be opened *free*, for a certain number of hours daily.

Every person presenting minerals should have his name recorded in the book containing the list of contributions, not only to verify the locality from which the specimen was obtained, but also to gratify people by a public acknowledgement of their labors, and thus stimulate other persons to send in specimens.

As *facts* are the sole foundation upon which practical Geology is based, it is of the first importance that the precise position and locality of each specimen, where possible, should be fully described, with the angle of dip, and direction by the compass. This valuable information should be succinctly recorded in the Catalogue of the Museum. It would add to the interest as well as value of the museum, if specimens of the manufactured article were placed side by side with the raw material—thus, a polished razor would be shown with the Londonderry iron ore. The varieties of the marbles and gypsums might be pleasingly exhibited by specimens of vases, candlesticks, and such like ornaments. Alongside of the ochres might be shown the different shades of Ross's Metallic Paints. The building stones should be cut into cubes six inches across, with the top polished and the sides dressed in different styles, and the bottom left in its natural state.

Copper, Lead, and other minerals would also have the other substances with which they are combined exhibited alongside of them, and thus induce the analytical student to search for substances that he might not otherwise have thought of looking for.

The agates, amethysts, and other beautiful stones and crystals which are collected on the shores of the Bay of Fundy, will add charms to the collection, no doubt, in the eyes of many, though, at the present time, we may not be able to apply them to any practically useful purpose. Above all, the fossils should be collected, and their localities and positions carefully noted down, for they are the index marks to guide us in our researches through the pages of geological history, which never mislead, but clearly mark out distinct areas and successive deposits, which are never reversed, although those found in some localities may be absent in the formation of the same class of rocks.

As far as he could learn from Dawson's work on Geology,

neither the older Pliocene, Miocene, Eocene, Cretaceous Wealden, Oolitic or Lias formations, averaging a thickness of 6,000 feet in Europe, have hitherto been found in Nova Scotia; and therefore, by the absence of so many geological divisions, the researches of the Nova Scotian are simplified when seeking for the type or name of any unknown specimen.

The temperature and character of springs are deserving of attention. Those of an unusually cold character are considered by miners as favourable indications of a lead deposit, while hot springs are found to flow from copper lodes. The chalybeate, containing carbonate of iron, deposit an ochreous scum, and it is a favorable indication of a coal or iron-stone formation. I have generally found the springs in Nova Scotia to be of a temperature of forty-eight degrees, while the mean temperature of the air is forty-two degrees.

The physical geography of a country will, to a certain extent, indicate its geological structure. A lofty or mountainous country, with barren, pointed summits to the hills, will indicate a granite formation, while deep ravines with precipitous banks, but with more vegetation upon their tops, are characteristics of the slates; the limestone and coal districts are marked by rounded hills or ridges, and the more modern clay and diluvial deposits (produced by the abrasion of the older rocks) are either generally covered by extensive forests or a fertile vegetation.

The limestone rocks are deserving of particular attention. It is to be observed that all the qualities of lime, whether rich, poor, or hydraulic, in any degree, assume indifferently any color: they may be either white, grey, yellow, buff or red. Such as yield from one to six per cent. of silica, alumina, iron, magnesia, either separately, or in combination, give rich limes upon being burnt. Limestone with silica in the state of sand, magnesia, oxides of iron, or manganese in various proportions but limited to between fifteen to thirty per cent. of the whole mass, yields poor lime.

Limestones containing silica in combination with alumina, (common clay) magnesia, &c., in various proportions limited to eight or twelve per cent. of the whole mass, yield moderately hydraulic limes; and when they contain more than twenty and up to thirty per cent. of the above ingredients, but the silica in the proportion at least of one-half, the limestone yields *eminently* hydraulic limes. The experiments upon which the above conclusions are based, show that limes owe their hydraulicity, or power of setting under water, to the presence of a certain quantity of clay, and sometimes, but rarely, to a certain quantity of pure silica. The stones containing much silica in the composition of the clay, swell in setting, and are likely to dislocate the masonry executed with them; those, on the contrary, in which the clay is in excess, are likely to shrink and crack. The magnesian limestones or Dolomites, appear to be the least exposed to these inconveniences. Limestones which contain more fossils are exposed to the inconvenience of producing a lime likely to slack at various and uncertain periods.

Berthier's mode of analysis was recommended, which is to be found in Wealde's Rudimentary Treatise on Limes and Cements.

Brick clays should also be collected and their per centage of sand recorded, which should be from fifteen to twenty per cent. of the whole mass. Pottery clays should also be sent in and samples of their ware obtained from the works at Dartmouth and the Truro road; this would answer the double purpose of being a show-room for the manufacturers, and stimulate them to improve their wares. Felspar is a large ingredient in our granite rocks, and therefore porcelain clays are likely to be found in their neighborhood.

PAPERS TO BE READ DURING THE SESSION
OF 1859–60.

Nov. 21, 1859.—The Pre-Columbian Discovery of America, Part I. Greenland. By ROBERT MORROW, Esq.

Dec. 5.—1. On some points of interest in the Geology of Nova Scotia. By J. W. DAWSON, L. L. D., &c., *Principal of Mc Gill College, Montreal.*
  2. Notice of Dr. Hamel's Paper, on the Invention of the Electric Telegraph. By HUGO REID, Esq.

Dec. 19.—The Variations of Temperature exhibited by Underground Thermometers. By Professor EVERETT, *King's College.*

Jan. 16, 1860.—Nova Scotia. By A. PILSBURY, Esq.

Jan. 30.—The Saxons of Germany—their Land and their Language. By Professor STIEFELHAGEN, *King's College.*

Feb. 13.—The Botany of the Carboniferous Rocks of Nova Scotia. By the Rev. D. HONEYMAN.

Feb. 27.—The Government System of Education in England. By HUGO REID, Esq.

March 12.—The Registration of Births, Marriages and Deaths. By the Rev. Dr. CRAMP.

March 25.—The Pre-Columbian Discovery of America. Part II. America. By ROBERT MORROW, Esq.

April 9.—Electric Currents. By ANDREW MACKINLAY, Esq.

April 23.—Recent Discoveries of Roman Remains in Britain. By W. GARVIE, Esq.

REPORT.

In conformity with the instructions of the meeting on the 4th of January last, at which the Society was formed, the Council then appointed hereby report their proceedings since that time.

Having, through the kindness of the Governors of Dalhousie College procured the free use of rooms at the College, the Society opened its first session on Monday, the 21st of February, 1859, when a paper was read by Dr. Cogswell on the KIND OF EDUCATION BEST ADAPTED FOR NOVA SCOTIA.

Meetings were held fortnightly thereafter till the beginning of May, at which the following papers were read:

March 7.—Notes on the Preservation of Timber Buildings from Fire.—By Lieut. HOME, R. E.

March 21.—Decimal Currency.—By the Hon. W. A. HENRY, M. P. P.

April 4.—The Fossiliferous Rocks of Arisaig, Sydney County.—By the Rev. D. HONEYMAN.

April 18.—Warming and Ventilation. — By W. S. SYMONDS, Esq.

May 2.—Certain new Minerals discovered in the Trap Formation, Bay of Fundy.—By Prof. How, King's College.

The advantages of Local Museums in Connection with Mineralogical Studies.—By H. POOLE, Esq.

With a view of diffusing a knowledge of discoveries and improvements in Science and the Arts, the Council ordered the following periodicals for circulation amongst the members:

The Edinburgh Philosophical Journal.
The Journal of the Statistical Society.
Silliman's American Journal of Science.
The Quarterly Journal of Agriculture.
The Mechanic's Magazine.
The Civil Engineer and Architect's Journal.

Through the kindness of the Secretary of the Smithsonian Institute at Washington, U. S., the Society has received six volumes of the transactions of that learned body.

At their meeting on the 25th of June, the Council resolved to print a small volume of "Transactions," giving an account of the origin and progress of the Society, a list of the members, a copy of the Regulations, and abstracts of the papers read during the session. The work is now at press and will be ready soon, when a copy will be sent to every member.

The Society now numbers *seventy-five* members. *Twenty-one* enrolled their names at the meeting on the 4th of January. These, with *sixteen* made members by being nominated to the Council, constitute the original members of the Society, *thirty-seven* in number. *Thirty-nine* have been admitted by the Council, on proposal by members; making in all *seventy-six* members.

The Council have to regret the death of one of their earliest members, CHARLES DICKSON, Esq., who enrolled his name on the 4th of January. This reduces the list to *seventy-five*, now on the roll. Of these, *sixty-three* reside in Halifax, and *twelve* in the country.

During the recess, the Council has prepared a code of rules for regulating the business of the Society.

REGULATIONS.—These, as has been mentioned, will be printed in the ensuing volume of transactions. (See page 10.)

FUNDS.—The state of the funds is as follows: the Treasurer had, up to the 30th November, received £35 due by members for the first year, £34 from members residing in

Halifax, and £1 from two country members. He had, on the order of the Council, expended £10 0s. 9d., having in his hands a balance in favor of the Society of £24 19s. 3d.

The items of expenditure are as follows :

Fuel, gas, &c., at Dalhousie College,	. . .	£2 5	0
Circular, with Society's Prospectus,	. . . .	3 0	0
Circulars announcing meetings, &c.,	. . . .	3 5	9
Collecting, ...	. . .	1 0	0
Postage, &c.	. . .	0 10	0
		£10 0	9

In conclusion, the Council think they may fairly congratulate the Society on the progress which has been made. One short session has already been held during which several able papers were read, including two—by Prof. How and the Rev. D. Honeyman—containing valuable original matter on the Natural History of the Province. The Council have been fortunate enough to procure twelve papers for the ensuing session on subjects of general interest and importance; and they are not without hopes that the Society's proceedings will have a highly beneficial effect in giving publicity to valuable information that might otherwise be neglected, discussing important questions, stimulating original research, and developing the genius, capabilities, and resources of the Province.

Read and adopted at General Meeting of members held on Saturday, Dec. 3d., 1859.

H. REID, } Secretaries.
W. GARVIE, }